Tales of
OAKAPPLE
WOOD

Jenny Partridge

Derrydale Books
New York · Avenel, New Jersey

CONTENTS

PETERKIN POLLENSNUFF

Peterkin Pollensnuff whistled loudly as he rode his bicycle along the riverbank. "I'm so hungry," he thought. "Maybe, if I hurried, I could finish my paper route and be back home in time for another breakfast."

He pedaled around a corner at great speed, and then suddenly swerved to avoid a huge snail that was lazily crossing the path!

The bicycle skidded, and crashed into a prickly bramble bush. Peterkin fell off, scattering newspapers everywhere.
"Creeping caterpillars!" he gasped, rubbing his head. The snail merely frowned at him and carried on. Peterkin pulled his bicycle from the brambles and saw, with a sinking heart, that the front tire had a flat!
"Oh no," he cried. "However can I do my paper route now?"

A large and colorful dragonfly brushed past him. "Hello, young wood mouse," she said, landing on a twig. "Why are you so sad on such a fine day?"

"Oh, Dorelia, my bicycle has a flat," muttered Peterkin, "and I simply must deliver these newspapers before school." He sniffed and swallowed hard.

"Hush now, there's no need to cry," said the dragonfly. "I'm not crying," snapped Peterkin. "I've - I've got a cold, that's all." "Well, if you cheer up and wipe your eyes, I shall do your paper route for you," the dragonfly offered. Peterkin blew his nose loudly. "Gosh," he giggled, feeling much better. "Won't everyone be surprised when a dragonfly delivers their papers!"

"Hmm, maybe," said Dorelia, preening her wings. "It would certainly help folks to realize just how useful dragonflies can be. Now, where do you want me to go?" Peterkin gathered up his papers and put the bag on her back. "Mayfly Manor first please," he said. "And then Mr Squint the mole, and last of all the Twitchers at Clover Cottage. You won't get lost, will you?"

"Get lost?" exclaimed the indignant dragonfly, "I shall be back before you can say 'Creeping caterpillars'!"

Tossing her gossamer wings, she flew off with the bag of newspapers streaming out behind her. Happily Peterkin began to fix his bicycle.

Dorelia zoomed up the pathway of Mayfly Manor, just as old Colonel Grunt set out for his morning stroll. "Good heavens!" he said, astonished as his newspaper landed on the ground.

He looked up and could hardly believe his eyes. His morning paper being delivered by a dragonfly? He must be imagining things. "Too much elderberry port, old chap," he told himself.

The dragonfly flew on and arrived at Mr Squint's house, where the old mole was busily polishing his windows.

A newspaper dropped out of the sky and hit him on the nose. "Good morning, Mr Squint!" called Dorelia.
"Well bless my soul!" he cried, adjusting his glasses.
On she flew, over Harebell Heath until she saw old Grandpa Twitcher in his garden.

"Grandma, quick!" he called, as his morning paper floated down towards him. He hobbled down the path, pointing up at the dragonfly. Not looking where he was going, his foot caught in a tangle of ivy, and he toppled over!

9

"What is going on?" called Grandma Twitcher.
"Up there," shouted Grandpa excitedly. "Look!
A dragonfly delivering the papers!" But by
then, Dorelia had flown away,
and the sky was empty.

Nonsense, whoever heard of
such a thing. You're getting
as silly as a snail," scolded Grandma
Twitcher, helping him to his feet.
"Come along and I'll make you a
nice cup of blackberry leaf tea."

The paper route finished, the dragonfly flew back over Bilberry Hill and
landed beside Peterkin.
"Goodness," she said as he helped her to take off the newspaper bag. "That
was heavy."

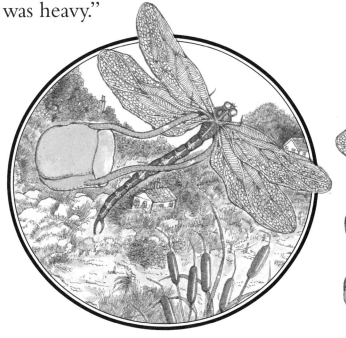

"Thank you, I really don't know what I would have done without you," said Peterkin gratefully.

"It was lucky I was passing," she remarked, "but now I must go. I have a thousand and one things to do today. Look after that cold of yours!"

The wood mouse smiled, and watched her fly over the tall grass, her wings glistening in the morning sun.

"I might have time for another breakfast after all," he thought, and he pedaled swiftly along the riverbank towards home.

RIFKINS

Rifkins, the badger, was drinking his early morning cup of tea when there was a knock on the door. Plop. A letter landed on the doormat. "It's from Cousin Quintin!" said Rifkins. "Arriving on Thursday at teatime," he read. "Why, that's today." The badger ran his paw along the dusty mantelpiece and sighed. "I shall have to clean this place from top to bottom," he said.

Unlike Rifkins, who was rather untidy and forgetful, Quintin was neat and elegantly dressed and kept a perfect house.
Rifkins set to work right away, scrubbing and cleaning and polishing.

Peterkin Pollensnuff and Verity Twitcher were passing just as a very dusty badger came out of the house sneezing loudly.

"You're busy, Mr Rifkins. Can we help you?" asked Peterkin.

"That's kind of you," answered the badger. "Any good at window cleaning?" Verity looked through the open window at the sink full of dirty pots and pans.

"You clean the windows, Peterkin," she said, "and I'll do the washing up."

Rifkins told Verity and Peterkin about Quintin's visit and how smart his cousin always looked. "Now I'd better go and find my best suit," he said. It was looking even shabbier than he remembered, so he hung it on the clothesline and beat the dust out with a carpet beater.

We'll go and get something for tea," said Verity and she and Peterkin ran off to Pollensnuff Stores.

The badger sank wearily into his chair. "Just forty winks," he told himself. But the grandfather clock ticked the time away and the next thing he knew, Verity was tugging at his sleeve.

"Wake up, Mr Rifkins," she said. "I think something awful has happened to your suit. It rained while it was on the clothes-line and we had to dry it over the stove."

"Do you think it will still fit you?" said Peterkin. Rifkins struggled into the jacket. It was so tight he could hardly breathe.
"It must have shrunk in the rain," he said.

"Either that or I've eaten too much of Mrs Twitcher's apple pie." He looked miserably into the mirror. There seemed to be more of him outside the suit than in it. He sat down and there was a loud splitting sound as a tear appeared in his trousers.

"Oh dear," he said. "Now what am I to do?"
Verity put her small paw in his. "Don't worry, Mr Rifkins, we'll get you some new clothes," she said. "Just lend us your wheelbarrow."
Mr Rifkins looked puzzled.

P eterkin and Verity took the wheelbarrow around to all the
woodlanders and told everyone how Rifkins had split his suit.
Before long they had collected some tweed trousers from Mr Squint and a
patchwork waistcoat from Grandma Snuffles.

L op-ear gave them some suspenders that he had been using to tie up his
runner beans and Jack Flax gave them a smart bowtie.

"H urry, Mr Rifkins," urged
Verity, when they arrived
back. "You've just time to change
before Mr Quintin arrives."
Rifkins was delighted when he
looked at himself
in the mirror.
"You both deserve
some blackberry
pudding," he said.

There was a loud knock at the door. It was Quintin. "My, how well you look, Rifkins," he said. "And where did you find that marvelous suit?"

"Oh, here and there," said Rifkins, "and with a little help from my young friends." But Verity and Peterkin could only smile. They were too busy eating pudding!

♥

JACK FLAX

Jack Flax, the hare, sat silently on his shoe-shine box. There had been no customers all day and he was bored. He gazed around at the sunny meadow full of summer flowers.

"Pretty as a picture," he murmured. "I'd like to paint them."

But Rifkins wasn't listening. "I am on my way to see Lop-ear. He has promised to mend that crack above my fireplace . . ." Jack was in too much of a hurry to wait, and Rifkins was left staring after him.

Jack hurried home. On the way he bumped into Mr Rifkins. "Hello there, Jack," greeted the old badger. "My, you're in a hurry. No shoes to shine today?"

"I'm not going to shine shoes any more," said Jack. "I'm going to be an artist."

18

Once in his cottage, Jack searched under his bed and pulled out an old box of paints.

As he opened the dusty lid, a moth flew out and startled him. The paints fell all over the floor.

"Bother," he said, picking them up and stepping on a tube of Sunshine Yellow.

He put the paints into a large bag together with some brushes and a pickle jar for a water pot. He pulled on an old smock and a beret, picked up his easel and hurried out of doors, leaving large yellow pawprints as he went.

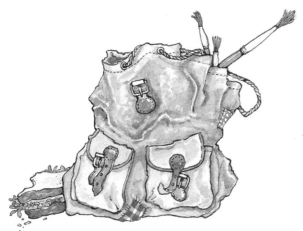

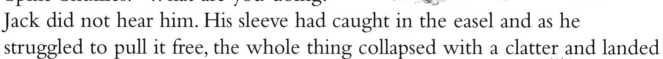

When he reached a small leafy glade he stopped to put up his easel.

Three little woodlanders appeared. "Good afternoon, Mr Flax," called Spike Snuffles. "What are you doing?" Jack did not hear him. His sleeve had caught in the easel and as he struggled to pull it free, the whole thing collapsed with a clatter and landed on his foot!

"Yeow!" he yelled, jumping about on one leg. The woodlanders giggled.

Then, with a splash, the water pot and all the brushes toppled over. Jack tried to catch them, but instead he slipped and fell into a puddle. The woodlanders giggled louder. "Go away," he snapped. "Can't you see I'm trying to be a famous artist?" And they scampered off.

20

J ack picked himself up and began again. When the easel was firmly standing, he pinned up a sheet of paper, took a brush and dipped it into the bright green paint.

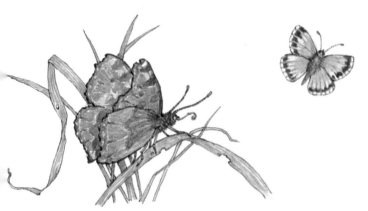

S ome butterflies gathered round him. Soon they were joined by a cloud of hoverflies. They buzzed loudly in his ear and tried to land on his nose to see what he was doing. Jack gave up. "Why can't they all leave me alone?" he said. And he sat down under a tree and munched a clover sandwich while he thought what to do.

V ery soon the drowsy warmth of the afternoon set him daydreaming.

21

While Jack dozed, the butterflies dipped their feet into the paint and chased the hoverflies across the paper.

A large spider, which had fallen into the open paintbox, crawled stickily after them, leaving a trail of crimson paint behind him. Then a family of grasshoppers hopped into the water pot and splashed everything.

Three loud excited voices eventually woke Jack.
"Marvelous!" Rifkins was saying.
"Such wonderful color," said Mr Squint admiringly, and Lop-ear agreed. Jack sat up and scratched his ear in amazement. Could they really be talking about his picture? Had his dream come true?

"Well done, old fellow," Rifkins declared, as he slapped Jack on the back.
"It's a masterpiece," added Lop-ear. Jack could hardly believe his eyes as he looked at his painting. Those few dabs of paint had become a field of poppies! How could he have done it? It looked splendid!

"Tell you what," said Rifkins, "I'll give you a whole sack of lettuce for it. What do you say?"
Jack was so astonished, he just nodded his agreement. "Where will you put it?" he asked.
"Why, I'll hang it over my fireplace," answered Rifkins. "It will hide that nasty crack I was trying to tell you about!"
And they all began to laugh.

CLARA QUINCE

"Mint tea, sugar, clothespins, antacid tablets." Clara Quince, shrew and housekeeper to Colonel Grunt, peered at the crumpled shopping list as she followed the path to Pollensnuff Stores.

To get into the shop she had to squeeze past a group of young woodlanders who were looking at a poster on the door announcing the Country Fair.

Once inside, she gave the list to Mrs Pollensnuff and sat down on a stool. "I see there's to be a Fair on Saturday," she said.
"Yes," said Mrs Pollensnuff. "The little ones are busy making costumes for the costume parade. I hope you will be bringing some of your special elderflower and gooseberry jelly again this year, Miss Quince?"

Clara smiled as she remembered the fairs of long ago, when she and her brothers had played on the carousels and swings.

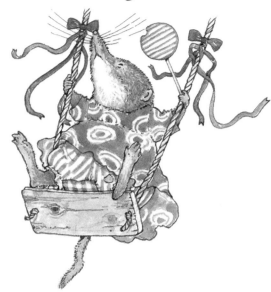

She remembered how excited she had been when she won a whole jar of colored lollipops, and the fun she had secretly peeping through a gap in the fortune-teller's tent.

"Pah, elderflower and gooseberry jam," she said picking up her basket. "I think I can do better than that!" And she hurried out of the shop leaving Mrs Pollensnuff to figure out what she meant.

"You've forgotten the antacid tablets," she called after her, but Clara had gone.

Back at Mayfly Manor, Colonel Grunt complained that Clara had not brought his antacid tablets and hiccupped all through supper.

When the table had been cleared and the plates washed and put back on the dresser, Clara crept up to the attic. She blew the dust and cobwebs off the old wooden chest that stood by the wall and looked inside.

She pulled out several lace tablecloths, nine curtain rings and a cracked goldfish bowl, took them downstairs to the kitchen and talked to Tarquin about her marvelous idea for the Fair.

He was busy toasting muffins and told her she should get on with her jam making. But instead, Clara fetched her sewing basket and set to work. She was going to have fun!

Saturday was sunny and everyone in Oakapple Wood was out enjoying the Fair. Little mice giggled as they lined up outside the mysterious fortune-teller's tent, jingling their pocket money.

Grandma Snuffles joined the line, dragging a reluctant Mr Squint with her. The crowd grew larger and Madam Columbine, the Fortune Teller, looked pleased as she awaited her first customer.

"You must beware of a strange three-legged creature with two heads," she warned Mr Squint. How amazed he was when he stepped outside the tent and collided with Amy and Pippin who had just been running in the three-legged race!

27

Colonel Grunt was the next customer. Madam Columbine gazed into her crystal ball and told him that if he looked inside his ear trumpet all his troubles would be over.

"Good gracious me," he said, pulling out a pack of antacid tablets. Grandma Snuffles sat down and peered eagerly at the fortune teller. "What do you see in your crystal ball for me?" she asked.

"For you, I see a pot of gold," said Madam Columbine. Grandma Snuffles was delighted – she couldn't believe her ears.

O utside, everyone was talking about the mysterious Madam Columbine. Who could she be? Where did she come from? At that moment the tent opened and the fortune-teller came out. There were gasps from the crowd as she took off her veil and headscarf.

"W hy, it's Clara!" said Colonel Grunt. Clara laughed so much that all her bracelets and rings jingled.

"B ut where is my pot of gold?" demanded Grandma Snuffles. Still smiling, Clara took a small jar from her pocket. On it was written "Madam Columbine's Elderflower and Gooseberry Jelly". Now everyone laughed, even Grandma Snuffles!

29

LOP-EAR

"It's those pesky caterpillars again!" Old Lop-ear gazed down at the cabbages in his garden. They were full of holes! He scratched his head, he wasn't likely to win any prizes at the Oakapple Show this year. Hopfellow called to him over the fence. "Hello there, Lop-ear! What's the trouble?"

"Caterpillars," muttered the old rabbit.

"I beg your pardon!" said Hopfellow.

"Caterpillars," he repeated.

"They've made a nice supper of my best cabbages!"

"Oh dear," said Hopfellow. "You'll not win First Prize at the Show with cabbages like that!"

"I know," sighed Lop-ear. It had always been his ambition to win First Prize on the vegetable stall.

"My grandfather used to put pepper on them," suggested Hopfellow. "Makes the caterpillars sneeze so hard they all fall off, he used to say!"

"Ah! Perhaps I should try that," said Lop-ear. "Thank you, Hopfellow."

He hurried inside his cottage and fetched the pepper shaker from the kitchen table. Verity Twitcher was passing by on her way home and giggled when she saw Lop-ear sprinkling pepper on the cabbages in his garden.

"Whatever are you doing, Uncle?" she asked. "Making caterpillars sneeze!" he replied.

She giggled again. "Whatever for?"

"Why, so I can win a prize at the Show, of course!" Verity shrugged her shoulders.

"Poor Uncle Lop-ear," she thought. "He gets sillier and sillier!"

Pleased with his work, Lop-ear put away his gardening tools and went inside his cottage. He cleaned his paws and sat down to eat a huge pumpkin pie for his supper.

Next morning he looked eagerly at the cabbage patch in his garden, but the cabbages looked even worse than they had the day before.

31

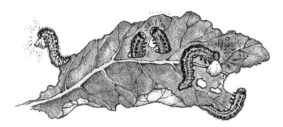

"Well, bless my boots," he said. "If those caterpillars have sneezed and fallen off, they've wasted no time in getting back up again! Whatever shall I do?"

"Morning Lop-ear!" Grandpa Twitcher called. "Having trouble?" "Caterpillars," said Lop-ear. "They won't stop eating my cabbages!" "Oh dear," said Grandpa, "and the Oakapple Show is on Saturday. Try a little vinegar - makes them thirsty, my old mother used to swear by it!"

So Lop-ear went inside and found some vinegar in his kitchen cupboard. He was busy sprinkling it all over his cabbages when he heard a giggle from behind the fence.

"Whatever are you doing now?" It was Verity again. "Making these old caterpillars thirsty," he said. She laughed.

"Poor Uncle Lop-ear, you're so funny," she said.
Still the caterpillars munched away at Lop-ear's cabbages, which now looked worse and worse. Old Lop-ear sat on his garden seat with his head in his paws. "What can I do?" he muttered to himself.

"It's my cabbages," he said, looking up. "The caterpillars keep eating them. I've tried giving them pepper to make them sneeze and vinegar to make them thirsty, but nothing seems to work."

He shook his head miserably.

Old Grandma Snuffles paused at Lop-ear's gate. She had been busy gathering rose petals to make her special jam for the produce stall. "What's your trouble, Lop-ear?" she asked.

"I'm not surprised," said the wise old hedgehog. "You treat those caterpillars with a bit of kindness and they'll be good to you - you mark my words!"

33

She wagged her paw. "Could you imagine your garden without butterflies? How dull life would be!" It was true, as he looked around his garden, butterflies of every kind danced about the flowers. What a lovely picture they made.

Suddenly he had an idea and rushed through his kitchen door.
He came back a few minutes later – with two sheets of paper and some charcoal.

On one piece he wrote in large letters

> *Caterpillars only*
> *- please _eat_!*

and on the other he wrote

> *Lop-ear's*
> *cabbages -*
> *please do*
> *_NOT_ eat!*

He placed one on each of his two rows of cabbages, and smiled to himself.

Next day, to his amazement, the row of cabbages marked Lop-ear's was untouched, without even the tiniest nibble, while the other row was still being hungrily eaten! By the end of the week his cabbages were large and luscious and Lop-ear looked forward eagerly to the local show.

Saturday dawned bright and sunny. Lop-ear whistled merrily to himself as he pulled up his biggest and best cabbage to take to the Oakapple Show.

The vegetable stall was overladen with carrots, turnips and enormous marrows, but everyone agreed that Lop-ear's cabbage was the most magnificent they had ever seen!

35

He was declared winner of the First Prize. Everyone clapped their paws and applauded as he was presented with the winner's silver cup. Lop-ear proudly held it high and as he took off the lid, out flew two beautiful butterflies! "Well bless my boots," he said, grinning, and he winked at Grandma Snuffles.

♥

HOPFELLOW

Hopfellow the frog was dozing contentedly in the sunshine on the riverbank when he was awakened by a sudden jerk on the end of his fishing line.

"My!" he cried, "this must be a big one!" He pulled hard, and out came an old boot covered in weeds. "Well, I can't cook that for my dinner."

The sound of giggling made him spin around. "Hello, young scallywags!" he called, as Verity Twitcher and the Pollensnuff twins, Amy and Pippin, appeared behind him. "What are you three up to today?"

"Nothing," they sighed. "We're bored."

"Bored?" exclaimed Hopfellow. "Why, when I was your age, I played on the river all day long!"

"But what did you do, Mr Hopfellow?" asked Pippin.

37

"Ah," replied the frog dreamily, "my cousin Quilp and I used to have the most marvelous boat races."

"But we don't have a boat," said Verity sadly.

"Come with me," cried Hopfellow, "and I'll show you how to make your own."

Under the tall horse-chestnut trees, several large prickly green shells lay on the grass.

"There," said Hopfellow, pointing to one. "Now, who could wish for a finer boat?"

Hopfellow showed them how to carry the shells on their heads, back to the river.

"I can't see where I'm going!" squeaked Amy.

The frog carefully fitted a long twig inside each shell boat to make a mast. "Now for the sails," he said. "Fetch me my newspaper, Verity."

38

"There you are, jolly sailors," he cried, launching the little boats. "In you jump!"

They scrambled into their shells, chattering happily to each other.

"Right," shouted Hopfellow from the bank. "First one to reach the bridge is the winner. GO!"

Using their paws as paddles, they splashed along, laughing and squealing.

"Out of my way, Pippin!" cried Amy, "or I'll bump into you."

Their little boats collided, and almost capsized. "Ugh," spluttered Pippin, "my tail is all wet – look out, here comes Verity!"

Hopfellow ran along the riverbank, calling, "Careful now Verity, don't lean over too far or you'll fall in."

Verity was a caterpillar's length in front of the twins, and paddling very fast.

"I'm winning," she shouted. "I'm the best sailor!" She bounced about excitedly, rocking the boat from side to side until suddenly it overturned, throwing her into the water.

"Help," she gasped. "Oh, help!"

Hopfellow grabbed his fishing line and raced to the little bridge. "Don't panic, Verity! I'll soon have you out of there."
He cast his line; the fish hook caught in the belt of her dress and he lifted her, dripping, out of the water.

The others stared at poor Verity as she dangled in mid-air. Hopfellow hauled her up on to the bridge, and put his coat around her. "I don't know what your Grandmother will say. You'd better come back with me and dry yourself."

The twins paddled to the bank, and climbed out of their boats. "Oh Verity, you did look funny!" giggled Pippin.

"Now, now," said Hopfellow, "I think Verity has learned her lesson! Come on back to my cottage for the finest tea you have ever had."
They all hurried to Hopfellow's house, snuggled under the water forget-me-nots.

Hopfellow made the tea and the children put their wet clothes by the fire to dry. "Ouch," cried Verity as Amy rubbed her with Hopfellow's roughest bath towel.
"I'm sure a large slice of blackberry pie will make you feel better," said the frog.

It was indeed a wonderful tea.
Afterwards Hopfellow lit his pipe and told them tales of his adventures on the riverbank.

It sounded so exciting that Verity
and the twins felt a little ashamed
that they had ever said they were
bored.
"I think it's time you went home
now," said Hopfellow when their
clothes were dry again.

"Oh," cried the twins, "can we come again, and sail our boats,
Mr Hopfellow?"
"Of course," smiled the frog, "but next time I must teach you to be better
sailors – what do you say Verity?"
"Atchoo!" she sneezed, and everyone burst out laughing.

HARRIET PLUME

"Phew!" Harriet Plume sat down wearily on an old tree stump. She mopped her brow and looked at the small pile of wild crab apples she had collected in her basket.

"Not enough here to make me fat," she sighed. The peace of the wood was broken by excited squeaks as the Pollensnuff twins scampered through the trees. "Quick Amy!" shrieked Pippin. "This way!" They ran straight into Harriet, nearly knocking her over. Ripe crab apples spilled from their satchels.

"Whatever is going on?" Harriet cried. Please Mrs Plume," gasped Pippin, "Sergeant Quilp is after us!" "Oh, what shall we do?" squealed Amy.

Sergeant Quilp came stumbling through the brambles. "There you are, you young devils," he began. "Oh! Good morning Mrs Plume." "Good morning Sergeant," said the squirrel. "What can I do for you?" Amy and Pippin trembled behind her skirts.

"Well, I'd like a word with these two mice. I've good reason to believe they have been stealing Colonel Grunt's apples!" "Ooh!" howled Pippin. Amy started to cry. "Nonsense," said Harriet, "I'm sure the twins wouldn't do that! There are plenty growing wild in these woods. You must be mistaken, Sergeant."

Quilp scratched his head, puzzled. "Well, if you say so Mrs Plume, but I could have sworn I caught sight of them up one of the Colonel's trees. I suppose I might be wrong. Mind you, if I catch these two scallywags anywhere near his orchard again, I'll tie their tails together!" He stalked off, muttering to himself.

44

"Wow!" said Pippin. "That was close, thank you Mrs Plume." They were just about to run off, but Harriet caught them both by the ear.

"Just a minute you two, not so fast," she said sternly. "You haven't really been stealing apples have you?"

They hung their heads. "Why, I should let you eat all these, and give yourselves tummy-aches, just to teach you a lesson."

"We're very sorry," said Amy in a small voice. "They looked so delicious - much bigger than the wild ones - we just couldn't stop ourselves. Please, don't tell Colonel Grunt or Sergeant Quilp!"

"All right," answered Harriet, "but you must make up for it."
"How Mrs Plume?" asked Pippin.
"You come home with me and find out!"

So they picked up all the apples
back to Acorns End. Once inside
and followed Harriet Plume
her little kitchen, she gave them
both aprons. Pippin's was a frilly one, and he looked so funny!
"You weigh the sugar," Harriet told him, "and you, Amy, wash the apples.
We are going to repay the Colonel by making him some crab apple jelly!"

They busied themselves,
squeaking all the time to each
other. Soon the water was boiling
on the stove and they watched
Harriet chop up the apples and put
them in the pan.
"Now, you make some tea Amy,
while I give this a stir, and Pippin!
Take your paws out of the sugar
bowl."

They all drank sweet blackberry
leaf tea and then Harriet put
the crab apples into a piece of
muslin. She hung it from a hook in
the beam, where the juice slowly
dripped into a large bowl
underneath.

Then she sent the twins to the garden shed to find some large jars.
"Bring them in, and polish them until you can see your naughty little faces in them," said the squirrel.
They rushed off excitedly and, sure enough, tucked behind some sacks of grain they found several empty jars.

"Oooh!" cried Amy. A large black spider was crawling out of the jar she was carrying, and she almost dropped it.

Harriet boiled the apple juice, mixed in the sugar and carefully poured it into the jars. "Can we try some now?" asked Pippin, smacking his lips. "Certainly not," cried Harriet, "you'll burn your tongue! But while it cools I'll show you how to make some pretty lids for the jars."

47

When the crab apple jelly was set, Harriet put three jars into her basket. "Come along, we are taking these to Mayfly Manor," she said. "And no dipping into the jelly on the way!"

"Why, Mrs Plume, what have we here?" asked Colonel Grunt as he opened the door. Harriet told him how the twins had helped her to make his favorite jelly and he promptly asked them all to join him for tea.

They sat down to little cups of sweet chamomile tea, thickly buttered oat-grass scones and, of course, crab apple jelly.
"Mmm," sighed the Colonel. He grinned at Harriet. "Tell me twins, where *did* you find such delicious crab apples?"

COLONEL GRUNT

Tarquin the butler paused at the gateway to Mayfly Manor. "I do hope the old Colonel will be all right," he said. "We've never left him for a whole day before."
"Don't fret," said his wife Clara the cook. "He can't come to any harm, and we shall be back before supper. Come along, Grandmother will be waiting for us."

Meanwhile, old Colonel Grunt was looking forward to a day on his own. "Tarquin's a good butler, but he fusses so. And fancy Clara telling me to keep out of her kitchen! Cheek! I'll prove I'm as good a cook as she!" he muttered. "I shall bake a cake for tea!"

Making up his mind, he banged his walking stick on the floor and headed for the little kitchen. "Now then, I shall need flour." He hobbled over to the shelf and adjusted his monocle. Yes, there it was. He put some into Clara's mixing bowl, with a few eggs. "Six should be plenty," he thought.

He added some butter and a tin of wild cherries, and stirred briskly. Bits of cake mixture flew about, sticking to his whiskers. My! this was going to be a cake to remember!

All at once his monocle fell off. "Now where on earth did that go?" he cried peering short-sightedly about him, but the monocle was nowhere to be seen. He put a paw into the mixture and tasted it.

"Hmm, I wonder where Clara keeps the sugar?" He squinted at the shelf. "Confounded monocle! I can't see a thing without it. Aha! This looks like sugar."

He tipped some into the bowl and continued stirring. "Old Squint and Grandma Snuffles are coming to tea - won't they be surprised by my marvelous cake!" he chuckled.

He put the mixture in a large cake tin and placed it in the oven. Feeling drowsy after all his hard work, he poured himself a glass of elderberry port, and settled down in his favorite armchair.

He was awakened some time later by the smell of burning! "Oh goodness me, my cake!" He scurried into the kitchen and pulled the smoking tin from the oven. "Confound it!" he cried. "Hmm, never mind, I can cover the burnt bits with Clara's chocolate icing. Then no one will notice."

The Colonel iced the cake and stood back to admire it. "Well done old fellow!" he said to himself. Just then there was a loud knock at the door, and wiping his paws, he went to welcome his two guests.

"You look different, Colonel," said Grandma Snuffles as she sat down in a large armchair in the parlor. "You're not wearing your monocle, and is that chocolate icing on your chin?"

"You'll have to speak up, my dear," Grunt answered. "I can't find my wretched ear trumpet!" "You're sitting on it," shouted Mr Squint. "What's that?" muttered the Colonel. "Ah! here it is, I was sitting on it! Now, how about some tea? I have a special treat for you both!"

51

He grinned at them as he went out. Moments later, he returned with a tray of wobbling teacups and the cake on a silver platter.
"What a magnificent cake!" cried Grandma. "Did your Clara make it?"
Grunt snorted. "Pah! Clara? Certainly not. I made it myself."
"Oh dear," whispered Mr Squint.

Grandma poured out the tea as Colonel Grunt proudly cut three large slices of cake. "Eat up, Squint old fellow," he urged. "There's plenty more!"
Mr Squint reluctantly took a bite. Suddenly he gasped for breath, and his glasses fell off! "Salt!" he spluttered.

"What's that?" asked Grunt. "Port? But I thought you were drinking tea!"
"The cake!" Squint cried, "there's salt in it!"

Grandma looked closely at the slice of cake she had been about to eat. "Whatever is this?" she asked, and she pulled out the lost monocle!

Grunt shook his head sadly. "I'm so sorry, my dear friends," he said. Somehow his beautiful cake had gone wrong!

"Never mind, Colonel," Grandma said, patting his arm. "Mr Squint and I thought your cake looked splendid."

Squint nodded, and wiped his sore mouth on his napkin. "It was a very nice thought," he added kindly.

53

"Promise you won't tell Tarquin or Clara," sighed Grunt, as he cleaned his monocle and put it back on. "They'll think I'm such a silly old vole."

"It will be our secret," said Mr Squint. "Grandma, is there any more tea? I can't think why, but I feel very thirsty!" Colonel Grunt could not help smiling. Tarquin and Clara returned that evening to the sounds of laughter coming from the parlor.

"Good evening Colonel," said Tarquin. "Is everything all right?"

"Capital, thank you," answered Grunt as he winked at the others. "We have had an unforgettable tea-party!"

GRANDMA SNUFFLES

Grandma Snuffles put down her knitting and sighed. "What a beautiful day," she said, as she took another sip of rosehip tea.

It had been a long, hard winter in Oakapple Wood and it was pleasing to feel the spring sunshine warming her once again.

"Morning Grandma!" called Mrs Plume. "Are you coming into town?" The hedgehog shook her head. "My old bones are too weary these days."

"Come come, it's springtime! I am going to buy a new hat. Why don't you come. That old one of yours looks as if the dormice have been nibbling at it!"

"Nothing wrong with my hat!" snapped Grandma." It's just a little old – like me!"

"Oh, stuff and nonsense!" argued Mrs Plume and went on her way.

"Pah, what a cheek," muttered Grandma. "Dormice indeed!" She took off her hat and studied it, then she shook her head slowly.

It did look rather old and battered, but she was very attached to it. "Perhaps I could brighten it up a little," she said thoughtfully. She wandered over to the riverbank where the cuckoo flowers grew. She picked a few and tucked them under the hat band. Then she spied some primroses and added these. She smiled at her reflection in the water. "A little water violet would be nice," she said and reached for a bloom. "Oh and some Columbine – it's so pretty!"

"Good morning, Grandma Snuffles!" called Mr Squint on his way into town. "Whatever has she got on her head?" he thought to himself.

56

"Morning Mr Squint, what do you think of my new hat?" she proudly asked.
"Er, splendid," said the mole politely. "Quite splendid!"
"Oh, do you really think so?" said Grandma excitedly, the tip of her nose going pink. Well fancy that - a compliment already! Squint shook his head and smiled.

Grandma was feeling quite light-headed. "I think I shall go into town after all. It would be a pity to own a hat as lovely as mine and not show it off!" She made her way along the path, stopping now and then to add a flower or two to the hat until she could hardly see where she was going. She felt like a young hedgehog again - all set for the spring parade! Proudly she walked into the town.

Suddenly there was a loud buzzing around her head as a large bumble-bee settled happily on a piece of honeysuckle on her hat. It was soon joined by another and then another until there seemed to be a whole swarm hovering above her.

"Go away!" she cried, beating the air with her stick. "Be off with you!" But they would not budge, and continued to follow the hat. By now an interested crowd of young woodlanders had gathered to view the strange sight.

"Whatever is that?" someone cried.

"Well, it looks like Grandma Snuffles – but what has she got on her head?"

Pippin and Amy Pollensnuff started to giggle, and soon everyone was laughing.

"Get off, I tell you!" Grandma cried.

"Go away, you silly creatures!" But still the bees followed her.

It was then she caught sight of the others laughing at her, and she blushed down to her last bristle. How silly to think that a few flowers could make her look younger.

She took off her hat and miserably hurled it into the bushes. Mrs Plume appeared by her side, and patted her arm.

"There there my dear," she said kindly. "You come home with me and we'll have a nice cup of tea together."

The woodland children felt very ashamed that they had laughed at the old hedgehog. "Whatever shall we do?" cried Amy. "Poor Grandma looked so upset." He picked up the hat and stared at it. "I've an idea!" said Pippin suddenly. "Come on Amy, and bring that hat with you!"
They ran off home to Pollensnuff Stores, and were soon busy with scissors and pins!

Meanwhile, at Mrs Plume's cottage, even the third cup of sweet-scented blackberry leaf tea could do little to cheer poor Grandma Snuffles.

"What a foolish old hedgehog I've been," she moaned.

"Nonsense," said Mrs Plume, refilling her teacup. "First thing tomorrow we shall go and buy you a new hat!"
Just then there was a loud knock and the sound of giggling. Mrs Plume hurried to the door but there was no one to be seen. On the doormat sat a large hat box marked GRANDMA SNUFFLES - special delivery!

She took it to the astonished hedgehog. Grandma carefully removed the lid. To her delight she found inside the prettiest hat you ever saw! It was covered in colorful ribbons with a pretty veil over the front - and not a flower to be seen!

She clapped her paws together excitedly "Ooh, whoever could have sent it?"
"Quickly, try it on," said Mrs Plume. "Beautiful, beautiful!" was all she could say. But there was something else inside the box!

She pulled out a jar, labeled Best Honey - With the compliments of the Bees of Oakapple Wood! "Well bless my old bristles. Put the kettle back on, Mrs Plume," laughed Grandma. "Today we have honey for tea!" Outside, hidden behind the hollyhocks, Pippin and Amy smiled as they heard laughter from the cottage. "Come on Amy, I'll race you home," said Pippin. "I could just eat a slice of bread and honey myself!"